Further Adventures of Tom and Huck

AND OTHER PLAYS

by Don Nigro

A SAMUEL FRENCH ACTING EDITION

SAMUEL FRENCH

FOUNDED 1830

SAMUELFRENCH.COM
SAMUELFRENCH-LONDON.CO.UK

ISBN 978-0-573-70258-7
www.SamuelFrench.com
www.SamuelFrench-London.co.uk

FOR PRODUCTION ENQUIRIES

UNITED STATES AND CANADA
Info@SamuelFrench.com
1-866-598-8449

UNITED KINGDOM AND EUROPE
Plays@SamuelFrench-London.co.uk
020-7255-4302

Each title is subject to availability from Samuel French, depending upon country of performance. Please be aware that *FURTHER ADVENTURES OF TOM AND HUCK* may not be licensed by Samuel French in your territory. Professional and amateur producers should contact the nearest Samuel French office or licensing partner to verify availability.

MUSIC USE NOTE

Licensees are solely responsible for obtaining formal written permission from copyright owners to use copyrighted music in the performance of this play and are strongly cautioned to do so. If no such permission is obtained by the licensee, then the licensee must use only original music that the licensee owns and controls. Licensees are solely responsible and liable for all music clearances and shall indemnify the copyright owners of the play(s) and their licensing agent, Samuel French, against any costs, expenses, losses and liabilities arising from the use of music by licensees. Please contact the appropriate music licensing authority in your territory for the rights to any incidental music.

IMPORTANT BILLING AND CREDIT REQUIREMENTS

If you have obtained performance rights to this title, please refer to your licensing agreement for important billing and credit requirements.

CONTENTS

FURTHER ADVENTURES OF
TOM AND HUCK

CHARACTERS

TOM SAWYER
HUCKLEBERRY FINN
BECKY THATCHER SAWYER

SETTING

Tom Sawyer's brownstone townhouse in New York city, in the year 1876. A sofa. A rug. A liquor cabinet. Tom, Huck and Becky are all now in their late thirties.

ABOUT THIS PLAY

FURTHER ADVENTURES OF TOM AND HUCK was first presented at Theatre NXS in Columbia, Missouri, on February 20, 2009. The performance was directed by L.R. Hults. The Production Stage Manager was Samantha Jones. The cast was as follows:

TOM SAWYER. . . . . .Bruce Humphries
HUCK FINN . . . . Jim McCrown
BECKY THATCHER . . . . .Jonna Wiseman

(Lights up on the interior of Tom Sawyer's brownstone townhouse in New York City in the year 1876. **TOM** *and* **HUCK** *are just entering.* **TOM** *is very well dressed.* **HUCK** *is down on his luck.)*

TOM. I knew right away it was you, the minute you said my name, but I just couldn't believe it. How the heck are you, Huck?

HUCK. I'm all right.

TOM. You look good. Well, you don't look that good. I guess a lot of people are down on their luck these days. When I saw you standing there in that alley, it was like I was dreaming. You know what I mean, Huck? It's been so long. I always felt bad about losing touch like we did. Gosh, it's great to see you. Wait till I tell Becky. You know I married Becky Thatcher, don't you?

HUCK. No.

TOM. You ever get married, Huck?

HUCK. No.

TOM. You're a wiser man than I am. You want something to eat? I can have the cook whip you up something. Ain't that a hell of a thing, Huck? We got us a French maid, a Dutch nanny, a German cook and a English coachman manservant flunky. Ain't this a great country? What do you want? A steak? I can have Gertrude whip you up a big thick one.

HUCK. A drink would be good.

TOM. Okay. What do you drink? Rye? Bourbon? Whatever you want, we got the best. I got to stock up a lot of liquor because Becky drinks like she's in some kind of a contest. Damn, it's good to see you, Huck. I thought you was dead.

HUCK. So did I.

TOM. *(pouring drinks)* So, did you have a good war?

HUCK. A what?

TOM. A good war. Did you have lots of great adventures in the war?

HUCK. No.

TOM. Many's the time I almost wish I hadn't got out of the war so early and went north, except in the end it turned out to be a regular gold mine, so who am I to argue with God's plan?

HUCK. God has a plan?

TOM. I figure he must have, some way or other, demented as it may seem.

(bringing the drinks over and handing one to **HUCK***)*

Here you go. Hope you like it. This stuff was made by a dead Scotsman. It's the best money can buy.

HUCK. What is it?

TOM. It's Scotch. I know it looks like horse piss and smells like varnish, but it's the finest in the world, trust me.

HUCK. No. God's plan. What's God's plan?

TOM. Well, how should I know? He's God. I figure he must have some sort of plan. I don't claim to know what the hell it is. *(holding up his glass)* Here's to the Queen's epiglottis.

*(***TOM*** drinks a sip. ***HUCK*** tries to down his in one gulp, then chokes and spits.)*

HUCK. Jesus Christ. This shit tastes like embalming fluid.

TOM. That's how you know it's the good stuff. You just spat about twelve bucks onto the antimacassar there. Becky's going to be mad as a cat with a hornet up her ass. You want some more?

HUCK. You got anything decent people drink?

TOM. We're rich now, Huck. We don't know any decent people. But let me take a look. *(rummaging in the liquor cabinet)* You come out of the war in one piece, looks like.

HUCK. Not exactly.

TOM. They didn't shoot off your balls, did they?

(**TOM** *finds another bottle.*)

HUCK. I ain't entirely right in the head.

TOM. Well, this is New York. You'll fit right in. Hell, Becky's crazy as a jay bird.

(**TOM** *pours* **HUCK** *another drink.*)

HUCK. Somebody always whispering in there. Can't make out what it's saying. I get spooked easy now. Owls. Wind rustling leaves in the trees, I get the shivers, can't stop shaking. Can't get warm. Can't sleep. Close my eyes, I see dead men in the woods. Eyes glowing like mold. Soil is ground up bones. I wake up and there's spiders on my face, brush one off into a candle flame, watch it burn. Bad luck. That's bad luck.

TOM. Uh huh. Okay. Have a drink. Sounds like you need it, pal. And drink it slow.

(*He gives* **HUCK** *the drink.* **HUCK** *sips this one.*)

You ain't the only person has bad dreams. I got this dream me and Becky are lost in the cave back home. We just keep walking through the cave, and I let go her hand for a second to scratch my ass and she's gone, down another tunnel, and I'm yelling for her, and I can hear her yelling for me. Then I come around a corner and there's this big cathedral like, with stalagmites and whatever, and in the middle of it there's Becky on her back on this big flat rock, naked as a newborn possum, and Injun Joe standing over her with his pants down, and I scream so loud I wake myself up, and when I wake up, you know who I find sleeping like a angel right there beside me in bed, Huck?

HUCK. General Sherman?

TOM. A sixteen year old whore named Lulu. She's dumb as a bucket, but man, does that girl know how to copulate. I don't even care that she giggles and farts while we're doing it.

HUCK. What about Becky?

TOM. No, Becky don't fart much, on account of she don't eat nothing to speak of. She just drinks. She farted up a storm when she was pregnant, though. Big as a damned hippo. It was like sleeping in the Congo. But me and Becky ain't had conjugal relations in a long time. She don't like it much, and she don't want no more kids. And seeing how ours turned out, I can't say I blame her. Anyway, all she ever did was lay there like a dead flounder anyhow. Well, the course of true love got a lot of sandbars in it.

HUCK. You always was a romantic guy, Tom.

TOM. I reckon I still am. I guess I'm just not the settling down type of person. War is hell, and marriage is war, and I'm the loser. Lord, I don't know what I was thinking. Well, that's not true. I know exactly what I was thinking. But once you get their bloomers off, what have you got?

HUCK. I don't know.

TOM. I don't know, either. (TOM *finishes his drink, pours himself another.*) So how'd you end up in New York?

HUCK. I heard you was here.

TOM. So you were coming to look me up?

HUCK. I guess.

TOM. Then what were you doing in that alley?

HUCK. I don't know. I get lost. My mind don't work right. I got shot in the head. I forget. Then I remember. And then I try to forget again.

TOM. Well, you and me sure got a lot of swell stuff to remember, don't we? You and me had some great old times on the Mississippi, didn't we, Huck?

HUCK. Yes. Like what?

TOM. Like that time we saw the murder in the graveyard, and that time they thought we was drowned in the river and we showed up at our own funeral. Or that time we went up in that balloon.

HUCK. What balloon?

TOM. The balloon. The balloon we went up in. That big hot air balloon.

HUCK. I don't remember going up in any balloon.

TOM. Sure you do, Huck. We sailed to Europe and had all kinds of Jules Verne type adventures.

HUCK. We never went up in no balloon, Tom.

TOM. You really must have got your head messed up good in the war, Huck, if you could forget that balloon ride.

HUCK. There wasn't no balloon.

TOM. We went to France.

HUCK. We never went to France, Tom.

TOM. Well, I sure as hell did. Got me some fine French beaver, too. You ever had a French woman, Huck?

HUCK. I don't think so.

TOM. I'll have to introduce you to the maid. That girl wiggles like a—

BECKY. *(a voice from off)* Tom?

TOM. Uh oh.

BECKY. Are you home?

TOM. *(calling offstage)* It ain't me, Becky. It's just burglars.

BECKY. *(entering, wearing a bath robe)* You been gone a long time. Did you get more liquor?

TOM. You already drunk all the liquor in this state. I had to go to Connecticut.

BECKY. *(looking at **HUCK**)* Who the hell is that?

TOM. Don't you recognize him?

BECKY. It's a bum.

TOM. It's not a bum.

BECKY. You've brought a bum into my house.

TOM. Becky, it's Huck.

BECKY. Who?

TOM. Huck.

BECKY. Huck?

TOM. Huck Finn.

BECKY. Who?

TOM. Huckleberry Finn. Our old friend Huckleberry Finn.

BECKY. Huckleberry Finn?

TOM. In the flesh.

BECKY. That's Huckleberry Finn?

TOM. Well how many Huckleberrys do you think we know, Becky? Huckleberry van Rensselaer? Huckleberry Schwartz?

BECKY. Huckleberry Finn is a boy.

TOM. He's our age, Becky. And he's been shot in the head, so you be nice to him.

BECKY. *(staring at* **HUCK***)* You're not Huckleberry Finn. You can't be.

HUCK. Okay.

BECKY. You look like some sort of a hired assassin.

HUCK. I was a soldier.

BECKY. You look awful, Huck.

HUCK. You look nice.

BECKY. I don't look nice. I'm getting carpet bags under my eyes.

HUCK. You're beautiful.

BECKY. *(taking that in, then heading for the liquor cabinet)* I need a drink.

TOM. Listen. I got to go out a minute to check on my simple-minded half-brother Sid down at the sausage factory. You remember Sid, Huck? Sneaky little pasty-faced nose-picking snitch? I let Becky talk me into letting Sid manage my sausage factory, which would have been a great idea except Sid's got the brain of a sand crab. We're getting in a shipment of Chinese pig heads tonight and he don't know what the hell he's doing. Becky, can you entertain Huck while I'm gone?

BECKY. *(pouring herself a drink)* What do you want me to do? Dance the hula?

TOM. Just talk to him. I know you can talk, because you ain't shut up once since we got married. Make him feel at home.

BECKY. You're going to leave me alone with him?

TOM. He's all right. Becky, it's Huck Finn. My best friend in the world.

BECKY. He looks like he just ate the baby.

TOM. Becky, he's standing right there.

BECKY. I know he's right there. I can smell him. And I don't want to be alone with him. He thinks I'm beautiful.

TOM. He don't know what he's saying. He was shot in the head. Wasn't you, Huck?

HUCK. I was shot in the head.

TOM. You just stay here a minute and drink your damned drink and I'll be right back.

BECKY. Fine. It's always been my girlish dream to entertain hobos while my husband's busy at the sausage factory.

TOM. Don't you mind Becky, Huck. She don't mean no harm. It's just twelve gallons of alcohol talking. I won't be gone long. I just bought this here sausage factory, and there's a lot goes into it. Of course, that's the beauty of sausage. You can put any damned thing in it and nobody knows the difference and it's still sausage. Now you just pretend like you're in your own home, and Becky can pretend she's normal. Damn, it sure is good to see you.

(**TOM** *goes. Pause.*)

BECKY. Will you stop staring at me?

HUCK. Sorry.

BECKY. What the hell happened to you?

HUCK. I was in the war.

BECKY. Tom was in the war, but he doesn't look like a buffalo herd ran over him.

HUCK. Tom was in the war about five minutes. I was there four years, if you count prison.

BECKY. Prison? You were in prison? So you're an escaped convict?

HUCK. I was captured. I was a prisoner of war.

BECKY. I'm sorry. I'm pretty rude sometimes. It's living in New York. Sophisticated people behave like animals. They just do it with cocktails.

HUCK. Animals are better than people.

(pause)

BECKY. So what are you doing here?

HUCK. Tom invited me up.

BECKY. But why did you come? Because if you think you're going to get any money from him, you can forget it. He won't give you anything. He never gives anything to anybody.

HUCK. I don't want money.

BECKY. Then why did you come? Because you think he's your friend? Anybody who ever trusted Tom Sawyer is in the poor house, the mad house or the charnel house.

HUCK. I came here to kill him.

BECKY. To kill him?

HUCK. Yes.

BECKY . You came here to kill my husband?

HUCK. I think so.

BECKY. Well, why haven't you done it, then? What's stopping you?

HUCK. I don't know.

BECKY. If you do it tonight I'll pay you. I'll give you everything I can lay my hands on. Just kill him. Kill him now.

HUCK. You want me to kill your husband?

BECKY. Well, maybe not right away. It'd be lovely if he could suffer for a while first. Make him suffer a few hours, and then finish him off. I'd have poisoned him a long time ago but I'm afraid the children would get into it.

They're all dumb as dirt. I don't like them much, but I don't want to kill them. I'm going to need somebody to take care of me when I'm too drunk to stand up, and Tom's sure as hell not going to do it. If I dropped over in a coma here on the rug, Tom would step right over me to pick up a nickel.

HUCK. You really want him dead?

BECKY. More than life itself.

HUCK. Why? What's he done to you?

BECKY. He's a monster. You can't imagine what it's like living with him. His brain is working all the time. He thinks in his sleep. He talks in his sleep. Sometimes he has long conversations with you in his sleep. I can't usually make it out. Something about the cave and pirates and some old marble he used to have. I don't know. He's insane.

HUCK. I don't think he's insane.

BECKY. He is. He's the craziest son of a bitch on the planet. He'll do anything for money. And not so much because he cares about money itself, or even what it can buy. He does, but that's not why. He's obsessed with the idea of it. Of treasure. Of getting. Of robbing. He doesn't just want stuff. He wants to take it from other people. He's the crookedest son of a bitch in the country, and that's saying a lot. Is that why you want to kill him? Did he cheat you out of something? He cheats everybody. He can't help it. He'd cheat a blind man out of his glass eye.

HUCK. You're drinking that too fast.

BECKY. I do everything too fast. That's my trademark. Speedy Becky. Speedy, speedy Becky. Hippety split on the trail to nowhere. Well, down the hatch and call me Grover.

(She drinks.)

HUCK. It's not good for you.

BECKY. That's the whole point.

HUCK. You want to hurt yourself?

BECKY. No, I want to kill myself, but I'm terrified of dying, so I decided to kill my husband instead. And God has heard my prayers and sent you here to do it for me. Do you need a knife? We've got a great set of carving knives in the kitchen. They were made in Bavaria. Tom took me on a tour of Bavarian sausage factories for our honeymoon. Them Germans wear funny short pants but they really know how to make a pig-sticker.

HUCK. I don't want a knife.

BECKY. Then how are you planning to kill him? You going to strangle him? Can I watch? Because I'd really like to see that. I want to see his eyes bug and his tongue flop out. I could make popcorn.

HUCK. Maybe I was wrong. I don't think too clear.

BECKY. No, no, you were right. Your impulse was right. Go with your impulse. That's what I always say. It's made me the woman I am today.

(She drinks.)

HUCK. I was sure before. But when I saw him, when we started talking, then after a while I wasn't so sure.

BECKY. Don't let him talk you out of it. He's got a line of bullshit as long as a garden hose. Don't be deceived by his charm. He's evil. I think he's the Devil.

HUCK. He's not the Devil.

BECKY. Then why do you want to kill him?

HUCK. I hear voices in my head.

BECKY. Well, kill him, and maybe they'll shut up.

HUCK. I don't know what to do. I should just go.

BECKY. Wait a minute. Let's talk about this. Maybe we can negotiate.

HUCK. I don't think so.

BECKY. If you'll kill him, I'll let you do it to me.

HUCK. What?

BECKY. You can do it to me twice if you kill him slow.

HUCK. Do what to you? *(He looks at her. Then his eyes widen as he gets it.)* Oh. Oh, Becky, you don't have to do that.

BECKY. But I will. I want to. I feel it's my Christian duty. Come on. We can do it right here on the rug if you want.

HUCK. Becky, he just went out for a minute.

BECKY. He says that, and then I don't see him for a month. We can do it in my bedroom. He never comes in there. Come on. It'll serve him right. We'll do it, and then when he comes home you can beat his head in with one of his god damned golf clubs.

HUCK. That wouldn't be right, Becky. You're his wife.

BECKY. That doesn't mean squat to him. Why should it mean anything to you? Come on, Huck. You know you always wanted me. You used to think about doing it to me all the time, didn't you?

HUCK. It don't matter if I did. Tom was my friend.

BECKY. You don't think he'd have screwed your girl friend if you'd had one? He screws anything that moves. He'd screw the neighbor's dog if it winked at him.

HUCK. I don't want to talk about this.

BECKY. You want to know a secret, Huck?

HUCK. I don't think so.

BECKY. Sometimes I have these dreams about Injun Joe. Injun Joe is doing it to me in the cave. In the middle of this big cavern. And I can hear Tom lost somewhere in the caves, calling out my name. And all the while Injun Joe is doing it to me. Injun Joe has a really big one, too. I'll bet you've got a big one.

HUCK. Stop it.

BECKY. You had a big one even when we were kids. I saw you and Tom splashing around naked at the old swimming hole. I'll bet it's a lot bigger now.

HUCK. *(holding his hands up to his ears)* You're scalding the inside of my brain.

BECKY. Tom just has a little bitty one, like a maggot, but he sure likes to use it.

HUCK. Becky, what happened to you?

BECKY. What happened to me?

HUCK. You were a nice little girl.

BECKY. What happens to anybody? Tom Sawyer happened to me. And it looks to me like he happened to you, too. Let's kill him before he happens to anybody else.

HUCK. I think about those times, that town, the river, those people, and it's like a dream.

BECKY. I dream a lot about rats.

HUCK. I close my eyes and I'm back there. Or on the river. I'm floating down the river in the fog with Jim.

BECKY. Jim who?

HUCK. My friend Jim.

BECKY. I don't remember any Jim. Did he have a big one?

HUCK. Stop it. I don't want you to be like this. I want you to be like you was before.

BECKY. I was like this before.

HUCK. No. You were a smart, funny, beautiful, nice little girl.

BECKY. That's what you saw. It wasn't what I was. You couldn't see what I was. You was too busy thinking about me naked. Men are all blind as bats and stupid as dog turds. Anyway, I grew up. We grew up. Everybody grew up.

HUCK. No. Not like this. This is wrong.

BECKY. Everybody grows up, Huck. That's a nice name. Huck. It's really fun to say. Huck. Huck. Why don't you just take your pants off and let's see how much you've grown up.

HUCK. I'm not taking my pants off.

BECKY. Aw, come on, Huck. Don't be shy. I've seen it before. I'd just like to see it again once before I die.

(She tries to get his pants off.)

No offense, Huck, but you smell like you just crawled out of the hind end of a cow. Maybe we could take a bath together first.

HUCK. *(trying to elude her)* Will you let go of my pants?

BECKY. I like it when you play hard to get.

HUCK. Becky, I mean it. Let go.

*(Trying to get away, with **BECKY** clutching onto his pants, **HUCK** falls over the end of the sofa, pulling **BECKY**, whose hands are trapped in his belt, down with him.)*

BECKY. Wheeeeeee.

HUCK. Stop it.

BECKY. *(on top of* **HUCK**, *still trying to pull his pants off)* Come on, Huckleberry. You know you want it.

HUCK. I don't want it.

BECKY. You can pretend I'm Jim if you want to.

*(**TOM** enters, stops, looks at them.)*

TOM. I got to hand it to you, Becky. When I tell you to entertain the guests, you entertain the guests.

BECKY. I'm trying to, but he won't let me get his pants off.

TOM. You might as well let her get your pants off, Huck. She's going to get them off sooner or later, anyway. She takes them for souvenirs.

BECKY. I love souvenirs. They're so much nicer than people. When we was taking the Bavarian sausage factory tour I got me a glockenspiel. You want to see it?

TOM. Becky, do you have to show everybody we know your glockenspiel? Nobody wants to look at your damned glockenspiel.

BECKY. *(staggering to her feet)* Fine. I'll just have another drink then.

TOM. Now there's a stunning plot twist.

HUCK. *(pulling his pants up and getting to his feet)* What the hell is the matter with you people?

TOM. We're just a couple of typical New Yorkers, Huck.

HUCK. You're sick. The both of you are sick.

TOM. I'm not sick. I feel okay. Do you feel okay, Becky?

BECKY. I'm on top of the fricking world. *(She drinks.)*

TOM. I want to thank you, Becky, for being so nice to my best friend.

BECKY. He came here to kill you.

TOM. No, Becky, I think that was you.

BECKY. I'm not kidding. He came here to kill you.

TOM. Huck didn't come here to kill me. He's my best friend in the world. Ain't you, Huck?

BECKY. He came to kill you. Ask him.

TOM. I don't have to ask him.

BECKY. Ask him, dumb ass.

TOM. All right. All right. Don't shit puppies. Huck, did you come here to kill me?

HUCK. Yes.

TOM. *(to* **BECKY***)* There. You see? *(It registers. Back to* **HUCK***.)* What?

HUCK. She's right. I came here to kill you.

TOM. That ain't a very funny joke, Huck.

HUCK. I'm not joking.

TOM. Why would you want to kill me? What did I ever do to you?

HUCK. You talked me into enlisting in the Confederate Army. You said it would be the greatest adventure ever. Then the first time we hear enemy fire, you desert and leave me there.

TOM. I didn't desert, Huck. I was just reconnoitering in the opposite direction.

HUCK. You took off like a race horse. I end up with a head wound in a prison camp and almost die, while you come north, get rich and sleep with Becky.

BECKY. You had your chance, Goober.

HUCK. How could you run off and leave me like that?

TOM. It was strategy, Huck. I just decided I could be a lot more use behind enemy lines.

HUCK. So I damn near get my head shot off and you go north and buy a sausage factory. Is that fair? Do you think that's fair?

TOM. This is America, Huck. What's fair is whatever you can get away with. That's the beauty of it.

HUCK. How did you get so damned rich, anyway?

TOM. Just good old American get up and go.

BECKY. He got rich selling worthless crap to the Union Army.

TOM. It wasn't all worthless crap.

BECKY. Yeah, some of the food was good for poisoning rats.

TOM. It was just me doing my part for the Confederacy, Huck. You was shooting Yankees, and I was selling them guns that exploded in their faces. In business we call that cutting out the middle man. Everybody helps the war effort in their own way. You see, Huck, that's the great thing about capitalism. You got your supply, and you got your demand, and the value of what you supply depends on the demand. There's a big demand in a war, so a war is a great place to do business. And that's what America is all about.

HUCK. America is not about that.

TOM. Yes it is, Huck. And if you'd paid more attention in school, instead of poking around all day at the old fishing hole, you'd know I'm right.

HUCK. You're not right. That's not what America is.

TOM. I don't see what you're getting so riled up about. I pull off a strategic reconnoiter and make a few bucks on the war and you want to kill me? That don't seem like a good enough reason to me.

HUCK. Jim is dead.

TOM. Jim who?

HUCK. Jim. My friend Jim.

TOM. I don't think I know him.

BECKY. They went down the river. He had a big one.

HUCK. Jim, that I went down the river on the raft with.

TOM. Oh, you mean Miss Watkins' Jim? What about him?

HUCK. He's dead.

TOM. Well, that's a shame, Huck. I always liked old Jim. We sure had some good times together, didn't we?

HUCK. He was my best friend.

TOM. I'm your best friend, Huck. I always been, and I always will be. Now, come on, let's you and me have a drink together and talk over old times on the Mississippi.

HUCK. I don't want a drink.

BECKY. I want a drink.

TOM. You've got a drink.

BECKY. *(looking at the glass in her hand)* Oh. *(She downs the drink.)* I want another drink.

TOM. I think you've had enough, Becky.

BECKY. Not if I'm still conscious. Am I still conscious?

TOM. Just barely.

BECKY. Then I need another drink. I'd get it for myself except I can't feel my knees.

HUCK. Don't you people care that Jim is dead?

BECKY. Poor Jim. He had a big one, and now he's dead.

HUCK. Shut up. Just shut up.

TOM. Don't tell my wife to shut up, Huck. That's my job.

HUCK. I'm trying to tell you that Jim's dead, and nobody is listening.

TOM. We're listening.

BECKY. I'm not listening. I'm hoping to pass out soon.

TOM. Shut up, Becky.

BECKY. Okey dokey.

> *(She collapses face first onto the sofa.)*

TOM. Oh, good. She's unconscious. I think I love her the most when she's unconscious. Now what was you saying about Jim, Huck? He had a big one?

HUCK. We come across a bunch of Yanks in the woods. We was shooting back and forth for a long time, then they took off running. And we come after them, and found a pile of dead soldiers there in the woods, and one of them was moaning something horrible. And I looked at him and I saw it was Jim. I could hardly recognize him. His face was half blowed off. I thought at first, Jesus, I just killed my best friend Jim. He finally gets himself free, and then I go and kill him in the woods. Then I saw his gun. The damned thing had exploded in his face. I got down on my knees and I put his head in my lap and tried to comfort him, but I don't know if he knew me or not. He said my name, but I don't know if he knew me. He thought we was back on the river, at the end. God, I wished we was. Then somebody shot me in the head and I woke up in a prison camp.

TOM. Well, Huck, that's an awful sad story, and I'm real sorry to hear about Jim and all. Honest I am. Jim was a pretty good fella, but after all, I mean, he was just a—

HUCK. What? He was just a what?

TOM. All I was sayin was that Jim was just a—

HUCK. He was my best friend.

TOM. I'm your best friend.

HUCK. I don't think you're anybody's friend. Jim was saving up his money to buy back his wife and children from the white people who owned them. He never hurt nobody in his whole life, and he was the best friend I ever had.

TOM. I'm sorry you got messed up in the war, Huck. But it ain't my fault. I didn't start no war. I was just trying to stay alive like everybody else.

HUCK. Hell, you probably made the damned gun that killed him.

TOM. Huck, guns don't kill people. People with guns kill people. I just sell people the guns. I don't make nothing. I'm a entrepreneur. That's French for rich American. And your friend Jim was trying to kill you, Huck. If that gun hadn't exploded in his face, he might have blown your brains out with it. You ought to thank me for saving your life. I should get a medal. Hell, I never had nothing against Jim. I got nothing against nobody. It's just business, Huck. That's all it is. It's just good old American business. That's why we fought the war in the first place. To preserve our sacred way of life and spread it around to everybody else and maybe make a few bucks on the side.

HUCK. That time me and Jim got back from on the river, and you played that trick on him, Jim thought you were the Devil. You remember that, Tom?

TOM. I sure do. We had some fun times with old Jim. He was a good sport.

HUCK. I think he was right. I think you are the Devil. Becky said it, too.

TOM. *(looking at* **BECKY**, *who's still face down on the sofa)* Yes, Becky's a world renowned authority on all theological matters. Also, she's still got just about the most beautifully formed pair of buttocks I ever seen in my life. *(squeezing her buttocks)* Here. Squeeze these once. She's squirted out four kids and they're still as firm as a cantaloupe. Her buttocks, not the kids. The kids is kind of squishy, especially in the cranium.

HUCK. You are. You are the Devil.

TOM. I ain't the Devil, Huck. I'm an all American boy.

(putting his arm around **HUCK**)

Now why don't you and me just sit down and talk about old times like friends.

HUCK. *(pulling away)* Get your damned hands off me. I'm not your friend. My friend is dead.

(**HUCK** *begins to cry. He can't stop. He sits down on the sofa beside* **BECKY** *and cries.*)

TOM. *(looking at* **HUCK,** *uneasy about the crying)* Well, now, there's no reason to bawl, Huck. I know the war can put a lot of bad stuff in a person's head, but you got to stay optimistic. You got to think about all the good times we used to have.

HUCK. It wasn't real. Nothing you and me did was real. It was all lies, like your damned balloon trip to France.

(Pause. **TOM** *watches* **HUCK** *cry.)*

TOM. Huck, you remember that marble spell?

HUCK. What?

TOM. That marble spell. You remember it? We did it when we were kids. You take a marble, put it in a box, bury it, say the spell, leave it there a while, and then when you dig it up, the box'll be full of all the marbles you ever lost. And if you got a big enough box, you can get back everything you ever lost—not just marbles, but everything. Baseballs and rocking horses and dogs and people and everything. But when I dug up the box, the only thing in it was just the marble I put in. Everything lost was still lost. I was so disgusted I throwed that marble away into the bushes. But then I got to missing it, so I went looking for it, crawling around most of a day on my hands and knees in the grass, looking for that stupid marble, because I missed it so much when it was gone. This taught me a profound lesson, Huck.

HUCK. What lesson?

TOM. That superstition is bullshit. Just like religion. And I'm a highly respected deacon in my church, so I ought to know bullshit when I see it. But what I been thinking about, more and more, Huck, is that someplace there's got to be a kind of an attic, somewhere, which is the place God stores all the stuff you ever lost. And if you could just find the door to that attic, and go up them steps, everything you ever lost in your life is waiting for you up there to find again. Sometimes I dream about that. I find a door in the house I never seen before, or maybe I seen a long time ago and then forgot about, and I open the door, and go up these steps to this attic, and there it is. Everything I ever lost in my whole life. And I just sit down there among all that stuff and I'm happy, Huck. I'm just completely happy.

HUCK. What do you want back?

TOM. Everything. I want everything back like it was. I want the town and the river and Aunt Polly and Becky and the cave and you and me and everything, just like it was. But then I wake up, and here I am with my drunk, insane wife, my brain dead kids, and my simpleminded half brother Sid screwing up my sausage factory. I been a big success. I'm rich. I get women. I get respect. Awards. I'm a personal friend of President Grant and half the criminals in his cabinet. But you know what I miss most, Huck? I miss just going fishing with you. That's what I miss. So I know how you feel, Huck. I really do. And I'm sorry. I'm sorry about your friend. I'd never do nothing to hurt you on purpose, Huck. You're the best person I ever knew in my life. I sure wish my kids was more like you. My kids are a bunch of goddamned pansies. They're more like Sid than me. If Sid had a pecker, I'd swear they was his.

BECKY. *(raising her head up briefly to speak)* They are his. *(She drops her face back into the sofa.)*

TOM. What?

BECKY. *(raising her head up again)* They're not your kids. They're Sid's.

TOM. They're not Sid's.

BECKY. They're Sid's children, Tom. Every one of them. Not yours. Sid's the father. We've been cheating on you for years. We do it every chance we get. Sometimes we do it in the sausage factory.

TOM. Sid? You been sleeping with Sid?

BECKY. Well, you've been sleeping with every whore on Broadway.

TOM. That's a lie. There's way too many whores on Broadway for any one man to get to in his whole life time. And Sid ain't never put his pecker in anything but a sheep.

BECKY. *(struggling to sit up on the sofa)* Sid hates you. You pay him next to nothing and treat him like a dog. Always sending him off to pay your bribes and do your dirty work. But I give him fringe benefits. I do it with Sid in your own house while you're off making money and screwing whores.

TOM. *(grabbing* **BECKY** *and shaking her)* The only whore I been with is you.

BECKY. Get your hands off me. Let me go.

TOM. I'll let you go. I'll throw you out the damned window.

BECKY. Huck. Help me. He's going to kill me.

TOM. I sure as hell ought to. Sid. Jesus Christ. Sid.

BECKY. Huck, do it now. Do it now, before he kills me.

HUCK. You better let her go, Tom.

TOM. *(shaking* **BECKY** *back and forth)* You let that limp-wristed egg-faced lip-diddler Sid into my bed?

BECKY. Well, why shouldn't I? You're never there.

HUCK. Tom. You're making her eyeballs jump up and down.

TOM. After I give you all this? After I saved you from Injun Joe in the cave?

BECKY. Injun Joe had me, too. He had a big one. Not like yours.

TOM. That's it. That's it. I'm gonna wring your neck like a Christmas goose.

(**TOM** *begins strangling* **BECKY**.)

HUCK. *(pulling* **TOM** *off* **BECKY**) Stop it. Stop it now, Tom. You stop it.

(**HUCK** *wrestles* **TOM** *backwards until they both fall onto the floor,* **HUCK** *seated on the floor and* **TOM** *on* **HUCK**'s *lap, with* **HUCK**'s *arms around* **TOM**.)

BECKY. You hurt my neck.

TOM. You're lucky I don't yank your damned head off.

BECKY. *(crawling off on all fours)* I'll get you for this, Tom Sawyer. You'll pay for this.

TOM. I already paid for it. I paid plenty for it. And what did I get? What did I get for my money? Nothing but heartache, heartache, heartache. *(pause)* This story is really messed up, Huck.

HUCK. Yes.

TOM. This train's gone off the track.

HUCK. Yes. What?

TOM. I know you think I got a glamorous life, Huck, but it's all crap. The government's damned near all rapscallions, and you got to bribe the hell out of everybody to make any money in this country. It's all money, Huck. They can talk till they're blue in the face about freedom and democracy and all that baloney, but that's just words. It's money. This country is all about money. But money don't fill you up. A person gets hungry for something else. I been having such bad dreams. I dreamed I was on this ship sailing in a drop of water, with these horrible monsters, bacteria and amoebas and such, floating in the great dark, coming to eat us. My whole life ain't worth a mouthful of ashes.

HUCK. It's okay, Tom.

TOM. How did everything get so messed up, Huck?

HUCK. I don't know, Tom.

TOM. America used to be such a great place.

HUCK. A place with slaves, Tom.

TOM. Well, okay, it's true, there was slaves, but it was nice. America was nice. For white people it was nice. White people with money, anyway. And even for kids like us with no money at all, it was a good place. We had the town. We had the river. We had the island. We had adventures. It was good then, Huck. Innocent. Free.

HUCK. Not for Jim.

TOM. And then the war come along and we all growed up and everything turned to shit. This ain't a good place any more, Huck. Something's killed it. Something's killed what was good in it. I can't take a whole lot of pleasure in it any more. Maybe you should kill me.

HUCK. I don't want to kill you any more, Tom.

BECKY. *(returning with a large carving knife)* Well I sure as hell do.

TOM. Becky, you put that thing down.

BECKY. What the hell are you two doing? Why are you sitting on his lap?

TOM. Just put the knife down, Becky.

BECKY. I'll put it down. Right in your aorta. I'm going to deposit this over-priced Bavarian pig-sticker about nine inches down your esophagus.

TOM. *(struggling to his feet)* You're not going to kill nobody with that thing.

BECKY. *(Rushing at* **TOM**, *slashing at him with the knife, chasing* **TOM** *around the sofa.* **HUCK** *remains on the floor as they run circles around him.)* Monster. Monster. Monster.

TOM. Hey. Cut it out, now. Becky.

HUCK. Becky. Stop it.

BECKY. *(chasing* **TOM** *around the sofa, the knife raised in both hands.)* I can't take it any more. If I hear that stupid story about how you got all those boys to whitewash the fence for you one more time, my head is going to explode. This is it. This is the end. Kill. Kill. Kill.

HUCK. *(standing up to try and get between* **TOM** *and* **BECKY** *as they run around the sofa)* Becky, will you cut that out and give me the–

*(***BECKY*** trips and falls, plunging the knife with both hands into* **HUCK**'s *chest. Brief pause.)*

HUCK. –knife?

BECKY. Huck?

TOM. Huck? Are you okay?

HUCK. *(looking at the knife sticking out of his chest)* Jim, could you pass me along another hunk of fish and some hot corn bread?

(**HUCK** *falls to his knees, then onto his side.*)

TOM. Huck? Hey, Huck? *(He puts his hand on* **HUCK**'s *neck.)* I think he's dead. Huck's dead.

BECKY. What was he talking about corn bread for?

TOM. He's dead, Becky. Huck is dead. He's dead.

BECKY. Well, I didn't mean to hurt him. I was trying to kill YOU.

TOM. *(holding* **HUCK**'s *head in his lap)* Oh, Huck. Poor old Huck.

BECKY. I didn't mean it, Huck. I liked him. He had a big one.

TOM. My friend is dead.

BECKY. Are they going to hang me now? Don't let them hang me, Tom. Please don't let them hang me.

TOM. Nobody's going to hang you.

BECKY. They're going to hang me. They're going to string me up like a beef carcass.

TOM. They're not going to string you up like anything.

BECKY. What are we going to tell them? Can we tell them you did it?

TOM. We're not telling them anything.

BECKY. But they're going to ask questions.

TOM. They're not going to ask any questions, because nobody's going to know.

BECKY. How can they not know?

TOM. He's a stranger, Becky. Nobody knows him. He's nobody.

BECKY. What are you going to do? Bury him in the garden? Dump him in the park?

TOM. No, Becky. That's not the right thing to do.

BECKY. We could throw him in the river. He'd probably like that. He'd like floating in the river. He liked the river. He was always talking about the river.

TOM. No. We're going to do this the right way. What we're going to do is, we're going to roll him up in the rug, and then I'm going to take him down to the sausage factory.

BECKY. The sausage factory? You're going to hide him in the sausage factory?

TOM. We'll just run him through the sausage machine. And in the morning it'll be like he never was here at all. Then we can remember him any way we want. There's no friend like a dead friend, Becky. And this way he don't go to waste.

BECKY. You're a very clever boy, Tom.

TOM. I know it. It's a curse.

(**BECKY** *sits down beside* **TOM,** *who is still tenderly cradling* **HUCK**'s *head. He rubs* **HUCK**'s *hair, tears running down his cheeks.*)

Poor old Huck. We sure did have some exciting adventures up there in that balloon. We sure had some good times, Huck. We sure did.

(*The light fades on them and goes out.*)

NOTEBOOK: FURTHER ADVENTURES OF TOM AND HUCK

1

In 1891, Mark Twain was planning a sequel to *Huckleberry Finn* in which Huck returned, sixty years old, from nobody knows where, crazy, believing himself a boy again, looking for Tom and Becky. Tom would return from wandering the world to find Huck and take care of him. They were to have talked of old times, two desolate old men, their lives a failure, all the beauty lost, and eventually die together. Twain never got around to writing it. He was a man with a teeming imagination and many unfinished projects. For him, writing was like groping about in the dark for something–you couldn't quite recall what. His structural sense, keen enough in shorter forms, tended to fail him in longer projects, and he would start things that broke off suddenly or trailed off into confusion. Some of his most interesting writing lies in his abandoned fragments, and some his best writing, as in *Huckleberry Finn*, has brilliant passages mixed with balderdash. Twain was a good writer, an awkward writer groping towards something quite unusual, a writer who's lost his way, and a great writer, often all in the same book. And the fact that he's all these things mixed together makes him more interesting, not less so. In the midst of this ragged disorder you can feel life throbbing. It is just like the disorder of God's brain.

2

When he was writing *Finnegans Wake*, James Joyce asked a friend to read *Huckleberry Finn* for him, and underline words and dialogue that had what Joyce referred to as European significance. The Irish hero Finn MacCool, Tim Finnegan of the ballad, and Huck Finn were related in Joyce's obsessively connective and aurally dominated sensibility. And like *Huckleberry Finn*, *Finnegans Wake* is a book in which the river is a major character, being both the River Liffy that runs through Dublin, and Anna Livia Plurabelle, the protagonist's archetypal wife.

3

In *The Adventures of Tom Sawyer*, Tom buries a marble in a box and recites a spell, believing that if he does so, all the marbles he's ever lost will be in the box when he digs it up again. But when he does, there's still just the marble he put in, and in disgust he throws the marble away, then repents and goes looking for it. The idea that one can somehow regain all lost beloved objects and persons is a powerful one. I have often dreamed of an attic in an old house in which I could find everything I once cherished, my childhood toys, comic books, lost books and other sacred objects, but also lost people and animals I loved, a place where I could go and play cards again with Grandma Nigro, while her tomato sauce boiled on a big caldron on the stove, or ask Grandpa Nigro about his life in Italy and his early days in America, or where I could sit down with girls I loved when I was younger. Dreams and memory are such a place, but neither are very trustworthy. You are just as likely to dream of things you very much do not want to experience, or remember things you'd like to forget. Art is the best way to revisit past beloved things. It's the attic I go up the steps into (or perhaps down the steps, because maybe that attic is really a basement, but we learn from Heraclitus that the way up and the way down are the same way) and re-connect with those magical lost things.

4

The other most powerful image, for me, in *The Adventures of Tom Sawyer*, is the cave Tom and Becky get lost in, where they encounter both treasure and intense danger. The danger lies in being lost itself, and in their budding sexuality, but also the Minotaur, in the form of Injun Joe. These caves form a labyrinth which is actually the subconscious not of Tom but of Mark Twain himself, who in turn was a manifestation of Sam Clemens, who was once a small boy on a river in a lost time.

5

Alfred North Whitehead says that art is the imposition of pattern upon experience, and the pleasure it gives lies in our recognition of the pattern, what Okkie Brownstein calls a perception shift. I am inclined to dislike the word 'impose,' and would prefer to replace it with 'discover,' except that to discover a pattern implies that the pattern is already there, which I suppose it is, not in the sense that God put it there on purpose but in the sense that every conceivable pattern is there waiting to be seen, or ready to spring into existence the moment we see it, like seeing Orion in the stars, or Charlie Brown seeing a ducky and a horsey in the clouds. Whitehead says, "Seek simplicity, but distrust it."

6

An artist helps an audience perceive connections between apparently unrelated things. Heisenberg says that often the most interesting discoveries occur at the convergence of two apparently unrelated lines of thought. The great artist or scientist is somebody who's capable of making these unlikely connections, finding unexpected doors in the walls of the labyrinth that lead one to other pathways. The joining of pathways is a node, like *Seven Dials*, where I once sat in a little restaurant one May afternoon, scribbling in a notebook, looking out the window, and talking to a pretty, shy French waitress, and had the uncanny feeling I seemed to be inhabiting several different times at once. Art is very much this sort of time travel.

7

The first thing is just to listen. You'll feel something itching inside your head. If you don't, sorry, mate, this ain't your racket. You feel the itching and you listen. And you write down what the voices say, and that's the start of it. And at first it might not make much sense, but that's all right, just like life. After a bit you have a mess of writing and you keep at it until you've found the story. Now, the story is a vast, vast, wonderland, and there's no end to it. Story goes on forever, see. You can start anywhere and follow a trail of story and it will lead you down this path or that path and there's never any end, because at any given node in the labyrinth you might always have taken another pathway that would have led you to another set of caverns. But at some point you'll decide that there's got to be some boundaries here, and that's when you begin tracing a line through that great twisted labyrinth of story, and that line is the plot, do you see? The story goes on forever but the plot is finite, the path cut through the jungle of story. Do you follow me, Cecil? Get away from those rabbits.

8

Extraordinary power of apparently accidental imagery stumbled upon in daily life, however dull and uneventful that life may seem. Deep, rich fuel for creation. It means something because you notice it. Eight deer. An old barn. A deserted brickyard. Twenty wild turkeys hobbling down a wet hillside. Numinosity is memory plus emotion.

9

Spanish pirates and whatnot. A man floats face down, a woman face up. There's camels and elephants everywhere. It's all done with enchantment. Faces, fishbelly white. It smells late. I dream about the river. Easy as cutting a pig's throat. A whole house come floating down the river with a naked dead man in it, shot in the back. You look at the moon the wrong way, it's bad luck, means death.

10

Elizabeth Bowen, speaking of her childhood, observes that it appeared clear to her that nobody who actually mattered was capable of being explained. The essence of poetic truth, she insists, is that no statement can be final. She also says she feels certain that if she could read her way back through all the books she read as a child, the clues to everything could be found. What a writer reads as a child scars and directs her forever.

11

Tom and Huck, archetypes of a largely but not entirely imaginary national self-image, the very clever boy with the devil in him, and the good hearted boy who triumphs over adversity and endures. We like to think this is what we are, and it's partly true. But pioneer America, an image of the unquenchable spirit of the poor and free, has an ugly underside: the massacre of the native inhabitants (Injun Joe's people), an economy built on the enslavement of other human beings (Jim's people), and the grotesquely stupid and ongoing destruction of the land and everything that lives on it. A writer doesn't decide upon the central obsessions of his work, but discovers them as he writes, over a period of many years. One of the deep threads of obsession that appears again and again in my work is what Joyce called the nightmare of history, particularly the nightmare of America's schizophrenic history. The Europeans come and take the land, massacring the native inhabitants as they go, butchering forests and buffalo and everything else that lives, fouling the land forever. The Revolution, its underlying principles of freedom and self-determination so admirable, perpetrated by brave men and genuine heroes who themselves either owned slaves or inherited wealth derived directly or indirectly from the slave trade, is in fact an entirely unnecessary shedding of blood: there was no revolution in Canada or Australia, and they're just as free as we are now, if not more so. The absurd bloody farce of 1812. The murderous jingoistic larceny of the Mexican War. The unspeakable carnage of the Civil War, an inevitable result of the obscenity of a slave economy. The monstrously stupid child of greed and ballyhoo that was the Spanish-American War. The comic opera horrors of the First World War, and the even greater nightmares it spawned: our history is constructed almost entirely of unspeakable, absurd and totally unnecessary mass slaughters, relentless bigotry and demented self-congratulation. There is much blood on our hands, and those who govern us continue to help engender and perpetuate the violent maniacs who want to destroy us. To read history, American history or anybody else's, is to despair for humanity.

CREATRIX

CHARACTERS

TIFFANY – a teenage girl
KIMBERLY – a teenage girl

SETTING

A bedroom late at night. All we can see are Tiffany and Kimberly, two teenage girls, sitting on the floor, in their pyjamas, thier backs up against the end of a bed, staring downstage, bathed in the eerie light of an invisible television set in a darkened room.

ABOUT THIS PLAY

CREATRIX was first presented at Theatre NXS in Columbia, Missouri, on June 19, 2009. The performance was directed by L.R. Hults, with sound by Bruce Humphries, set by David Summers and Linda Smith. The Production Stage Manager was Samantha Jones. The cast was as follows:

KIMBERLY ....Laura L. Brinegar
TIFFANY ....Kate Hamlett

(TIFFANY and KIMBERLY, two teenage girls, sitting on the floor in their pyjamas in the dark, bathed in the eerie television light of a downstage TV set that is invisible to us, as the tape they've been watching rewinds.)

TIFFANY. God, that was so awesome. I never get tired of watching it.

KIMBERLY. It's better than sex. Especially fellatio.

TIFFANY. Anything is better than fellatio.

KIMBERLY. How many times have we seen it?

TIFFANY. We've seen it a hundred and thirty-seven times. The movie. Not fellatio.

KIMBERLY. That many? Are you sure?

TIFFANY. I keep careful records of all significant world events in my diary.

KIMBERLY. This movie makes me happier than anything in the world.

TIFFANY. I know. It's like the first time you see it, you love it, but it puts you off balance. You've got to see it again. Then the second time, you think maybe you might get bored, but you realize there's things you missed that you want to see again. And the third time you see it, it's like you get to the other side of boredom, and start noticing all kinds of amazing details, like the furniture and the plants and things going on in the background, and you watch it again, and you watch it again, and it's like you're falling deeper and deeper inside it, like down the rabbit hole. It's like astral projection, except it's better, because we can do it together. It's a country we can visit on the same passport. It's like telepathy. Like the colors in my head are in your head, too. It's this other world, and you can go there any time you want, and nothing else is real. It's like going into the ocean, or into the womb, or someplace you were before you were born, like there are levels and levels of dreams, and you descend into the dreams, one inside the other. And it's so real, after a while, it's like you suffer when they suffer, but it's so beautiful, it fills you with this weird joy. After you watch it so many times, it feels like you made it yourself. You've become the creatrix.

KIMBERLY. The what?

TIFFANY. The creatrix. The goddess of all creation. It's like visiting the City of Lost Dreams in the middle of the Amazon jungle and scraping away an old vine from the pedestal of a statue and finding your own name written there and remembering suddenly that you're the one who built it.

KIMBERLY. Wow. That's deep. You're deep, Tiffany. You're so deep, my mother thinks you're a bad influence on me. She thinks you read too much to be a normal person. She's such a moron. Sometimes I just want to kill her.

TIFFANY. It doesn't matter what your stupid cow of a mother thinks. Nobody else exists. Our stupid parents don't exist, our stupid teachers don't exist. Nobody else can understand. It's pointless to even try to communicate with them because they're only listening with their ears. They'd think we were possessed by demons or something. They'd burn us for witches if we tried to explain the beautiful fog we live in when we watch this movie. This movie is like a big house you can wander in forever. It's like a memory theatre, where each scene is a room, like the haunted castle where the gods live, where unspeakable acts are performed, over and over, like beautiful naked rituals. It's like the place you see when you look in the mirror in my stepfather's house in the room where the mirrors reflect each other from opposite walls, so that you can see rooms that open up into other rooms forever. It's more real than copulation because it includes copulation. It includes everything. Sometimes I see it when I close my eyes, just before I go to sleep, and it gets all mixed in with dreams. Like last night, I dreamed I was swimming naked in a pond, by my stepfather's house, and there was a hurdy gurdy playing, and a crocodile swam up and ate me.

KIMBERLY. Gross.

TIFFANY. No. A certain amount of suffering is necessary for your art. Your own suffering, and sometimes the suffering of others. It's like being Vivienne.

KIMBERLY. Who?

TIFFANY. The girl in that poem we read in English class. Merlin is an older man who desires her, and he knows she's hungry for knowledge, and she cleverly persuades him to reveal to her, one by one, all his secret magical powers and spells, and then uses them to trap him inside a tree trunk forever. It's like that.

KIMBERLY. How is it like that?

TIFFANY. Because the movie is like a secret formula or spell that gives us power over them.

KIMBERLY. Over who?

TIFFANY. Over all of them. All the ones who want to order us around, tell us we can't see each other any more, put vile objects in our mouths and make us do unspeakable things. It gives us the power to do unspeakable things to them.

KIMBERLY. How does it do that?

TIFFANY. Because every time we watch it, we grow stronger.

KIMBERLY. I do feel stronger.

TIFFANY. What we need to do now is, we need to become them. We need to become those girls in the movie.

KIMBERLY. Do you mean the actresses? Or the characters they play? Or the people the characters were based on?

TIFFANY. Yes. All of the above. I want to enter the Fourth World, like Juliet and Melanie, and sleep with James Mason and Mario Lanza and Orson Welles.

KIMBERLY. Except of course they're all dead.

TIFFANY. Not in the movies.

KIMBERLY. But we're not in the movies.

TIFFANY. We could be.

KIMBERLY. That's unlikely.

TIFFANY. All the best things that could happen are unlikely. Love is very unlikely. I mean really intense, deep, supernatural love, which is a reality that's experienced in a part of the brain that most people don't even know they've got. But we know it. You and me. Just like the girls in the movie. Let's be them. I'll be Juliet.

KIMBERLY. You always get to be Juliet.

TIFFANY. Because I am Juliet. My father is a rectum who designs nuclear bombs. I have come to New Zealand to recover from life-threatening respiratory ailments. I have on more than one occasion seen the face of death.

KIMBERLY. So have I. I have infected bones in my legs. My pus must be drained with great regularity. It's made me delicate. But secretly I'm strong. Stronger than anybody could possibly imagine, just looking at me.

TIFFANY. Once I was Shanghaied to the Bahamas, where the natives observed me unclothed. I was deeply traumatized. And then, every night, in my childhood, the bombs fell on London. Plus my mother is fucking somebody on the side.

KIMBERLY. Actually, that's my mother, in real life.

TIFFANY. It's everybody's mother, Kimmy. Life is tragic for a woman.

KIMBERLY. But on the bright side, you live in a magic castle.

TIFFANY. Yes, but all castles are infested with rats. A large rat comes into my room in the night and does unspeakable things. And my mother knows, and looks the other way.

KIMBERLY. I wish I could leave my family and be your sister. My father sells fish. Mother takes in boarders. They observe me unclothed through keyholes. I have been violated by the young boarder. His penis is a deeply unsavory instrument.

TIFFANY. To console ourselves, we take baths together, then curl up in bed like cats. I love to watch you fall asleep. You make noises like puppies.

KIMBERLY. Years later, when our astonishing Victorian mystery novels are published, we'll become very famous, move to Scotland and have intercourse with Mario Lanza. Me first.

TIFFANY. Both at the same time.

KIMBERLY. But what if Mario Lanza is already engaged to some stupendously gorgeous movie starlet with ostentatious bezongas?

TIFFANY. If he is, then we'll be morally obligated to kill her. We'll strangle her naked in her bath, in a scene worthy of Hitchcock and DePalma. For the greater good of humanity. For art's sake. With Mario Lanza singing *Pagliacci* in the background.

KIMBERLY. He's so dreamy. He's my chocolate soldier.

TIFFANY. When my parents threaten to take me back to London, my near-fatal respiratory illness returns. You never leave my bedside.

KIMBERLY. I'm loyal unto death.

TIFFANY. We write passionate letters that Orson Welles will publish when we're dead.

KIMBERLY. Then you find your mother in bed with a stranger.

TIFFANY. They're drinking tea, naked except for the whipped cream on her nipples, and on the end of his penis. Hello, I comment, cleverly.

KIMBERLY. Then you begin to giggle uncontrollably.

TIFFANY. I suppose you will now require some sort of explanation, says Mummy, wearily, like Tallulah

Bankhead at the gynecologist. But I require no explanations. Sophisticated beyond my years, I have learned that all explanations are lies.

KIMBERLY. We're in love, she says.

TIFFANY. But what about father, I say?

KIMBERLY. He knows all about it. We'll all live together like civilized people.

TIFFANY. Oh, no, not that. Not civilized people. The most unspeakable crimes on the face of the earth are committed by civilized people. We much prefer the primitive races, because the savage mind is closer to the sensibility of the true artist.

KIMBERLY. So they conspire to send you to South Africa, to be trampled by ostriches.

TIFFANY. Life would be so much simpler if our mothers were dead.

KIMBERLY. Do you mean in the movie, or in real life?

TIFFANY. What's the difference?

KIMBERLY. If my mother knew I was letting you crawl in my window late at night and watch videos with me, she'd give birth to goats. She thinks you're mentally disturbed.

TIFFANY. In real life, or in the movie?

KIMBERLY. Both.

TIFFANY. Why couldn't your mother just die? People die every day. Why couldn't she?

KIMBERLY. Because what you want to happen never does.

TIFFANY. It does in the movie. Statues come alive and talk, and four foot butterflies suck honey from gigantic flowers, and we do a three way with Mario Lanza, who sings *Pagliacci* when he ejaculates.

KIMBERLY. In the movies, maybe. But not in Ohio.

TIFFANY. Why not in Ohio? How could we kill her? Let us count the ways. We could beat her over the head with a sand bag.

KIMBERLY. Or a brick. We could put a brick in a stocking.

TIFFANY. We'll invite her to tea, then lure her out to the park. I'll drop a pink stone along the pathway. Your mother will stop to pick it up. This will be the signal for you to commence whacking her violently over the head.

KIMBERLY. It's the day of the happy event. What fun. We had a jolly lunch at home, then took Mummy to tea, after which we bludgeoned her to death on the footpath. It was rather more difficult to do than I'd expected. I was hitting her and hitting her for quite a long time, until the brick came through the stocking. There was ever so much blood. But once having struck the first blow, a girl must keep going.

TIFFANY. I helped.

KIMBERLY. You were very helpful. My arms were getting tired.

TIFFANY. We struck her a total of forty-five times. I keep careful records in my diary.

KIMBERLY. It's such a beautiful story.

TIFFANY. Let's do it.

KIMBERLY. We just did.

TIFFANY. No, but I mean, for real. Let's do it for real. Let's kill your mother.

KIMBERLY. We can't kill my mother.

TIFFANY. Why not? They did in the movie.

KIMBERLY. But that's a movie.

TIFFANY. But it's based on actual events. A movie is also real. At the still point of the turning world, art and life become one. My stepfather's an artist. He taught me. Art explains the world to us. It is immensely valuable that way. Art provides moral instruction. We can create a world and then live in it. We can force upon circumstance our own reality. You are the carnival queen and she is the property horse, and it's high time the old nag went to the glue factory. We can become our own movie. All that's needed is the one bold act to pierce the veil. It's the triumph of art.

KIMBERLY. But it wouldn't be the same.

TIFFANY. I don't see why not. We know how to do it. We've seen it a hundred and thirty-seven times. Only the perception of the observer changes. The movie itself is eternal. Make your life a movie. Be the director. Choose your reality.

KIMBERLY. But there wouldn't be talking statuary and giant butterflies.

TIFFANY. Why not?

KIMBERLY. Because those things don't really exist.

TIFFANY. They do if we have good special effects people. Art is what enables a person to become one with the great universal creatrix. The goddess of all creation. Come on, Kimmy. Let's kill your mother. It'll make such a wonderful movie. We'll win Oscars. I've already prepared my acceptance speech.

KIMBERLY. You really are insane, you know?

TIFFANY. All great art springs from frustrated love, and what is love but the madness of desperation? We'll fashion a masterpiece from our mutual love. We will enter into the ecstasy of the animals, the pure, naked joy of creation. What do you say?

(Pause. They look at each other.)

KIMBERLY. Would I get top billing?

TIFFANY. Our people can negotiate all that.

KIMBERLY. Would I get to sleep with Mario Lanza?

TIFFANY. Unless you'd prefer Orson Welles.

(pause)

KIMBERLY. You're serious.

TIFFANY. Art is a very serious business.

(pause)

KIMBERLY. I think a person would need to believe very much, to make such a movie.

TIFFANY. People believe. They'll believe anything. They pray to a loving God who sends infants to hell and allows fathers to molest their children. We can make up a better religion than that. We can transform ourselves into the goddess. Put your hand on my heart.

(She takes KIMBERLY's hand and puts it on her heart. Then she puts her own hand on KIMBERLY's heart.)

Can you feel it? Can't you feel the great creatrix of the universe throbbing and seething and writhing beneath our flesh? She's dying to get out. It's our duty to release her. Are you with me? Because if you're not with me, nobody is.

(Pause. They look at each other.)

KIMBERLY. Where can we get a brick?

(They look at each other. The light fades on them and goes out.)

DRURY LANE

CHARACTERS

JAMES RUMPLEY – perhaps forty
JANE ARMITAGE – early twenties

SETTING

The stage of David Garrick's Drury Lane Theatre in London, at some point in the mid-eighteenth century. A piece or two of drab and worn, dark furniture, perhaps, but nothing fancy. The stage is mostly bare and the players are surrounded by darkness.

(Lights up on the stage of Drury Lane Theatre. **JAMES** *Rumpley looks to be about forty, tall, powerfully built, once good looking, now a bit gone to seed, and* **JANE** *Armitage, early twenties, still lovely but with some hard times visible on her face. Empty theatre, late at night.)*

JAMES. So. Shall we rehearse?

JANE. We're always rehearsing. We never cease to rehearse.

JAMES. Except when we're performing.

JANE. There's very little difference, really.

JAMES. Nevertheless.

JANE. I've grown weary of rehearsal.

JAMES. We must rehearse or we'll never get it right.

JANE. It will never be right.

JAMES. We must get it right, or Garrick will dismiss us.

JANE. He won't dismiss us. He likes us.

JAMES. He likes you.

JANE. He likes you, too.

JAMES. He likes me, but he doesn't trust me. He finds me unreliable. Unpredictable. And nearly undirectable.

JANE. So do I.

JAMES. You don't trust me?

JANE. I have trusted you far too much in my life, and look where it's brought us.

JAMES. It's brought us to Drury Lane.

JANE. Everything brings us here. Everything ends up here. All things come to Drury Lane.

JAMES. Do you think I trust you?

JANE. I don't care.

JAMES. You do care.

JANE. I just want to rest.

JAMES. We can't rest. We must rehearse.

JANE. I've forgotten my lines.

JAMES. You haven't forgotten anything. You never forget anything.

JANE. It's you who never forget. You're a monster of remembrance. And you torment me.

JAMES. I torment you?

JANE. You know you do.

JAMES. And why do you think I torment you?

JANE. Because you're a fool.

JAMES. You're the one who went to Garrick.

JANE. He was our friend.

JAMES. You went to him behind my back.

JANE. I had no choice. You were too proud to go yourself. We needed his help.

JAMES. And he was kind enough to offer it.

JANE. He was very generous.

JAMES. And what did you give him in return?

JANE. Nothing.

JAMES. *(his fury bursting out suddenly, an accusation, grabbing her arms)* WHAT DID YOU GIVE HIM IN RETURN?

(They look at each other for a moment. Then he lets her go.)

Was that too much, do you think?

JANE. It's always been too much.

JAMES. I think so, too. I can feel that it's too much. So why can't I seem to stop myself from doing it that way?

JANE. You've always been the victim of passions beyond your control.

JAMES. And you're one of them.

JANE. One among many.

JAMES. The only one that ever mattered.

JANE. If it pleases you to tell yourself that.

JAMES. You know it's true.

JANE. Then why do you torment me?

JAMES. Because you went to Garrick.

JANE. Garrick might have saved you.

JAMES. Nobody is saved. We're all damned here.

JANE. You might have been saved. You were too proud to accept his help.

JAMES. I didn't need his help.

JANE. We needed his help. Your child needed his help. But you preferred to turn thief.

JAMES. Preferred? I preferred? Do you imagine I had a choice?

JANE. You had a choice, but your pride prevented you. Pride, and drink, and falling into low company.

JAMES. Low company? Falling into low company? I'm an actor. I AM low company.

JANE. You know the company I'm referring to.

JAMES. I was raised by carny people, for God's sake. I travelled in gypsy wagons with a freak show. And yet you professed to love me. An undirectable man. An actor twice your age. Why, with this multitude of faults which you never tire of enumerating, why in the name of God did you ever want me in the first place?

JANE. I don't know.

JAMES. Well, make something up.

JANE. Mr. Garrick frowns upon improvisation.

JAMES. Another reason he can't stand me. I've been making it up as I go along all my life. I am a hopelessly improvisational individual.

JANE. You're a fine actor when you put your mind to it. But some spirit of perversity gets into you and–

JAMES. I'm not the one who sold her soul for a few pieces of silver.

JANE. YOU'D RATHER BE A THIEF THAN ASK A FRIEND FOR HELP. YOU'D RATHER HANG FROM A

GALLOWS. AND LOOK AT THE CONSEQUENCES. YOU'VE SACRIFICED YOUR WIFE AND CHILD TO YOUR STUPID, SELF-DESTRUCTIVE PRIDE.

JAMES. Now, that's too much.

JANE. It's the truth.

JAMES. It might be the truth, but it's too much. It sounds like a play.

JANE. To you, everything is a play. You've made yourself the tragic hero of your life, and your child suffers for it.

JAMES. I don't want to hear you preaching to me about my child.

JANE. I don't care what you want to hear.

JAMES. No, I expect you don't. *(pause)* Where is he now, I wonder?

JANE. He's gone across the ocean, to America.

JAMES. Gone to live amongst the savages, has he?

JANE. He's your son. What would you expect?

JAMES. What's he doing there?

JANE. Probably drinking and whoring, like his father.

JAMES. One can only hope. *(pause)* I don't like this scene. Can't we do something else?

JANE. We can't change it now.

JAMES. Why can't we? Who's to stop us? Garrick? Do you think old Garrick would try to stop us from rewriting this scene a bit?

JANE. We can't rewrite the scene. We can only play it.

JAMES. So you're enjoying it, are you?

JANE. I hate it. I just want to rest. But there is no rest for us.

JAMES. What about the seduction scene?

JANE. Oh, God, no.

JAMES. Why not? It's the best scene in the play.

JANE. It's too painful.

JAMES. You seemed to be enjoying it while it was going on.

JANE. I was a fool.

JAMES. Yes. You were a fool. An innocent girl from the country, come to London to be on the stage.

JANE. Stop it.

JAMES. The theatre, you know, child, does not have the greatest reputation as a place of high moral character.

JANE. I don't want to do this.

JAMES. You're improvising, Jane. Garrick wouldn't like that.

JANE. Do you slander your own profession? Then you slander yourself.

JAMES. I'll be buried in unconsecrated ground, and so will you, if you choose this for a life. You're better off to leave now while you still can.

JANE. I can't. My family will disown me. I've nowhere else to go.

JAMES. Yes. We are all drawn here by our desperation. I have loved and hated much in this place. All innocence is deflowered here.

JANE. It seems to me a very innocent place, in fact. A kind of holy place. Can you work here and not feel that?

JAMES. What do you want from this, girl? Do you want an easy life? Because you'll work like a dog. Do you want to be loved? Because one night they may seem to love you, but you can't take that love home with you, and the next night they'll be calling for your head on a platter. Do you want respect? Because you'll be viewed as a whore by respectable people everywhere.

JANE. Is that how they view you?

JAMES. Of course it is. A whore is paid to counterfeit an act of love. That's exactly what we do.

JANE. Do you enjoy destroying all my hopes? Hurling mud upon my dreams?

JAMES. Your hopes are unreasonable. Your dreams are not real. This sordid profession will use you up and kill you.

JANE. Then what are you doing in it?

JAMES. For me, the theatre is an exquisite form of suicide.

JANE. Then I've come here to die with you.

(They look at each other. He kisses her, very tenderly. Pause.)

JAMES. You're right. We must not do the seduction scene.

JANE. Why not?

JAMES. It was the scene of your deflowering.

JANE. By you.

JAMES. Yes, God help me.

JANE. We've begun the scene. We might as well finish it.

JAMES. No. I've changed my mind.

JANE. You can undress me, and bed me on a pile of costumes.

JAMES. No. I don't want to.

JANE. Come on. We must rehearse. You said we must rehearse.

JAMES. I was weak. I should have driven you away.

JANE. You tried. I wouldn't listen. I wanted you. I wanted this. I still want it now. Do it again now. Do it again. Deflower me.

JAMES. It's a thing that only happens once.

JANE. Not in the theatre.

JAMES. Get away from me. Have you no shame?

JANE. I married you. There's your answer.

JAMES. I remember you said to me after, lying together naked, you said, When I die, I want to haunt this place.

JANE. Did I say that?

JAMES. A theatre is a very dangerous location. A person must be careful what they say there. You say it, and then it happens to you.

(pause)

JANE. Do you think this is Hell, then?

JAMES. No. Too drafty. Purgatory perhaps. And yet you know, there could be worse things. Worse punishment, if this is that.

JANE. What we've done is our punishment.

JAMES. I think what it is. I think at the moment of death, love sets going these strange loops in the brain. And they play over and over. Because all love leads to suffering, and suffering feeds off itself, it makes strange loops, and one gets trapped in them. There's no help for it. It's the play one is cast in. The dead haunt, and in turn are haunted. All places are haunted. But theatres are the most haunted places of all. That's why we come.

(pause)

This is the play. I was a carnival boy who became an actor. You were an innocent girl from the country, come to the theatre. We made love on this stage one night. You were with child. I drank away what little we had. I was too proud to ask Garrick for help. You went and I hated you for it. I became a thief. I was caught and hung. You watched my public hanging with our son. And then you died.

JANE. And then I died.

JAMES. And the boy stowed away on a boat and went across the ocean. And here we are. Rehearsing the play. Again and again. Forever, in this place.

JANE. When I die, I said, I want to haunt this place.

JAMES. And so you have. And so you do.

JANE. It's a rather beautiful story, actually.

JAMES. Do you think?

JANE. We might make a play of it, you and I.

JAMES. We might. We have. We will.

JANE. There are worse fates than this.

JAMES. I expect. *(pause)* Do you think our son will be an actor?

JANE. Of course he will. Everybody is.

JAMES. Then God forgive him. And God forgive me. Or, the hell with God. Will you forgive me?

JANE. At the end of the play, perhaps.

JAMES. So. Shall we rehearse?

JANE. We're always rehearsing. We never cease to rehearse.

(They look at each other. The light fades on them and goes out.)

THE LITTLE PEOPLE

CHARACTERS

O'MULLIGAN – an old Irishman

SETTING

O'Mulligan sits in a wooden chair and speaks in a circle of firelight, surrounded by darkness.

For Marnie

(Lights up on **O'MULLIGAN**, *an old Irishman, who sits in a chair in the firelight, surrounded by darkness, and speaks to the audience.)*

O'MULLIGAN. But you were asking me if I'd ever had any acquaintance with the Little People. Ah, yes, the Little People. I love the Little People. I've seen the Little People many times, you know. Oh, yes. It's true. Mostly they like to keep to themselves, of course, but on occasion they've been known to grow fond of a house and hang about the place for years. Our Little People like to creep in the basement windows and move about the house at night. The Little People are surprisingly domestic, once you've earned their trust. I often leave little temptations for them at various places around the house before I go to bed. They like dark chocolates, creamed corn, and apple sauce. The Little People are very fond of apple sauce. I don't know why, exactly.

And they're a bit mischievous, as well. Sometimes, late at night, when I'm watching the television, the Little People like to sneak into the room and change the channel. I drift off to sleep in the middle of *Law and Order* and when I wake up, it's *Tom and Jerry*. The Little People love cartoons. They have quite a sense of humor, they do. Once I woke up and they'd painted my tallywhacker green. And they drew a little face on top. It's true, I swear. I got up in the dark to do what no man can do for me, and when I turned on the bathroom light, and saw a green pecker with a little smiley face looking up at me, I was so astonished, I peed all over the wall.

I'll tell you something about the Little People, though. They're good. Deep down, the Little People are good. Don't you believe those lies that some malicious and misinformed persons like to tell about them. The Little People are actually very, very good. The women are exquisite little creatures, so delicately formed, with such lovely dainty arms and hands. And they love their children dearly. They have beautiful little children. The Little People have quite tender emotions. I know it for a fact. I have heard the Little People, on more than one occasion, way in the dark middle of the night, sobbing their hearts out for some private grief a creature like us couldn't begin to imagine.

Oh, dear, how I love the Little People. The Little People are so very, very good. And around Christmas time, every year, what we like to do is, we set out the dark chocolates they simply can't resist. We put the dark chocolates in mouse traps to catch the Little People. We're often awakened, in the Christmas season, by the sound of the traps slamming shut, and the squeals of the Little People as they're caught. And if they're not dead, it's a simple matter to twist their little heads until the necks snap, to put the poor creatures out of their misery. Then we fry them up in a little butter, and, oh, are they delicious. Especially the women and the little babies. Their little heads crunch like walnuts. Oh, yes, I love the Little People. I do. But I prefer enchiladas.

(**O'MULLIGAN** *smiles, thinking about enchiladas. Blackout.*)

THE TALE OF MR. McGREGOR

CHARACTER

MCGREGOR – an old man

SETTING

A walled garden.

(**MR. MCGREGOR**, *an old man, speaking to us from his walled garden.*)

MR. MCGREGOR. Life here in this walled garden would be paradise were it not for the god damned rabbits. The woods in back of the garden is full of rabbit holes. The rabbits squeeze under the gate and eat my lettuce, they eat my French beans, they eat my radishes. They eat my parsley, they eat my cucumbers, they eat my cabbages. They eat my onions. I grab the rake and scream, STOP! THIEF! but they always seem to get away.

They're always here, always watching. I chase them, but they hide from me. I hear them sneezing behind the flower pots in the tool shed. Sometimes I hear them laughing at me. When I hoe my onions, I can feel their eyes on me. I can hear them giggling at me under the cabbages. Mrs McGregor tells me to forget them. But I can't. It's my lettuce. My cabbage. I feel so violated. I've grown so tired. I can't sleep. All I can think about is rabbits.

I try and step on them, but they elude me. I got one, once. Squashed his skull with my hobnail boot, and had the Missus bake him up in a pie. Rabbit pie. I hate rabbit pie. It was dreadful, disgusting, made me gag. But I ate as much of it as I could, anyway. Just on principle.

These rabbits. It's very disturbing. They talk to the mice. I swear to you, the rabbits talk to the mice. They've been spreading lies about me. And they seem to have taken to wearing clothing. I've found little rabbit shoes in my garden. Little rabbit jackets. Little red cotton pocket handkerchiefs. Little rabbit clogs. Clogs? These rabbits wear clogs? Do the rabbits clog dance at night under the moon with the owls? And why don't the owls eat them? It's a conspiracy. One carries a cane and smokes a pipe, for god's sake. I made a scarecrow out of their clothes once. But they came in and took them back. They have an agreement with the crows as well. They're all against me. All the rabbits and the birds.

There's a white cat in the garden that watches them. It doesn't chase them. It just watches. I don't even know whose cat it is. I don't know where it comes from. I don't know where it goes. I don't know what it means. It watches them, and then it looks at me. Why does it look at me? It's not our cat. Our cat is a fat, stupid brindle cat who sleeps all day on the bricks.

The rabbits sit and stare at me from the flat top of the wall at the bottom of the wood. And they're getting more aggressive. The other day, one of them attacked the cat. Not the white cat. Our big old fat cat, that sleeps on the bricks. They jumped on it and scared the living daylights out of it. The cat's been hiding behind the butter churn ever since. There's something wrong with these rabbits. These are not normal rabbits. They carve their names on the tool shed. Flopsy. Mopsy. Peter. Benjamin. I believe these rabbits have been sent by some malicious force specifically to torment me. I've tried to discuss this with my wife, but she thinks I'm ill. I can tell by the way she looks at me. But I'm fine. I'm perfectly fine. It's the rabbits. The damned Satanic rabbits.

Sometimes they hang about the rubbish heap outside the garden wall, smoking cigarettes and drinking with the squirrels. I can hear the drunken squirrels singing, "Who's been digging up my nuts? Who's been digging up my nuts?" I believe they are planning my demise.

Once I found six fat little baby bunnies, sleeping under a pile of clippings at my rubbish heap. I reached out and carefully plucked them up, one by one, and put them in a burlap bag. One, two, three, four, five, six fat little sleepy baby bunnies. I hung the bag on the wall while I went to put away the mowing machine. But when I brought it in to show the wife, so she could cut off the heads and skin them, she looked in the bag and said, "This is not bunnies, McGregor. This is a bunch of rotten fruit."

"It isn't fruit," I said. "It's bunnies. One, two, three, four, five six fat little baby bunnies I put in the bag myself, from off the rubbish heap. Let's cut off their heads and skin them." She emptied out the bag. It was three rotten marrows, an old blacking brush, and two decayed turnips. "If this is a joke," she said, "it isn't funny."

"It's not a joke," I said, looking in the bag. "It was bunnies. Six bunnies. One, two, three, four, five six fat little baby bunnies from the rubbish heap, to cut off the heads and skin." "Well, now they're turnips," she said.

"Don't you see?" I said. "This proves I'm right. It proves they're not normal rabbits. They've got the mice to eat a hole in the bottom of the sack, and pulled the bunnies out, and put in the turnips and the blacking brush. Don't you see?"

"You're a very sick man, McGregor," she said, and walked out of the room. Then I heard a snicker and looked up, and saw a row of bunnies sitting on the windowsill, laughing at me. I threw the turnips at them through the window. I hit one and broke the glass with another. The wife was fit to be tied. She's been having conversations on the sly with the doctor. I know what she's about.

I lie in my bed awake most nights, staring at the ceiling. I look at the window. I can see little rabbit heads, chins on the windowsill, little paws beside the chins, staring at me, red rabbit eyes. One night my wife will forget and leave the window open. And then the rabbits will swarm over the windowsill and into my bedroom, onto the bed, to get me. Or maybe she won't forget. Maybe she's in with them, too. They have had enough cabbage and roughage, you see. They have come for their revenge. For these are carnivorous rabbits. They come in the night to devour me. They plan to drag me out of my bed, kicking and screaming to their rabbit holes, and there dismember me with little rabbit knives, and bake me in a pie.

I lie in bed and wait for them. I hear something rustling at the window.

Help me. Somebody help me. Help me.

(The light fades on him and goes out.)

DOCTOR SINISTRARI ON
ZOMBIE ISLAND

CHARACTERS

DR. SINISTRARI – a very sinister looking gentleman,

SETTING

Dr. Sinistrari speaks to the audience from the fog.

DOCTOR SINISTRARI ON ZOMBIE ISLAND was first presented at Theatre NXS in Columbia, Missouri, on June 19, 2009. The performance was directed by L.R. Hults, with sound by Bruce Humphries, set by David Summers and Linda Smith. The Production Stage Manager was Samantha Jones. The cast was as follows:

DR. SINISTRARI .... Rory O'Carroll

(The sound of a foghorn in the darkness. **DOCTOR SINISTRARI** *appears from out of the fog.)*

DOCTOR SINISTRARI. Welcome to Zombie Island. I am the evil Doctor Sinistrari. I have locked you in my cabinet of horrors. It does not matter that Aquanetta cannot act. She is unspeakably beautiful, and perhaps can be persuaded to keep her mouth shut, except for the inevitable screaming, when we rip off her blouse. Wake up Lugosi and tell him to go fuck himself. I am that part of him that will endure as long as there are morons.

You may wonder if you are dreaming. Of course you are. But who has put the dream in your head? Not God. God is rotting in the compost heap with chicken bones. I have put the dream in your head. I, Doctor Sinistrari. Worship me if you dare. I will be behind the set, trying to screw Aquanetta. She moves with all the grace of an imperfectly wound simulacrum.

The sound in this movie is very poor. You can hear rustling in the background like a fire burning, but don't be alarmed. It is only the nitrates disintegrating the film.

In our scenes together, Aquanetta spends the whole time staring at my left ear. Why does she look at my left ear when she acts? Because she is afraid to look me in the eyes. She fears I will turn her into a zombie. Or, she fears I will see she has no idea what the hell she's doing. And yet she is a very nice girl, the sort of girl you'd like to bring home to Mother in a cardboard box.

The zombies are having a picnic. They have platters of meat, most likely human. The prop department appears to have dismembered some of the extras.

You may wonder how I, Doctor Sinistrari, a man of my extraordinary attainments, have managed to end up here on Zombie Island, in the ass hole of the world. It's actually a very amusing story which I shall perhaps relate on my death bed. Then I'll close the lid of the coffin and begin decomposing. Actually, I began decomposing in 1937. I have left instructions that I am to be ground up in a sausage machine to prevent my becoming a zombie myself.

I would not be a zombie for anything in the world. Sitting around all day in a darkened movie theatre, watching crap like this. No, not for me. Not for Mrs Sinistrari's little boy. I am surrounded by zombies. This is my punishment for coming to America. Hollywood is of course the zombie capital of the universe. There are more zombies on Sunset Boulevard than in all of Haiti.

But my island does have some advantages. The monkeys are rather amusing. I play checkers with them in the afternoon. George Zucco once tried to take two monkeys home in his suitcase. The results were catastrophic. Apparently monkeys suffer from claustrophobia. Who knew?

In my time, I have worked with all the greats and near greats here on my island. Boris Karloff. ZaSu Pitts. Sophie Tucker. Senor Wences. Warren G. Harding. Steamboat Mickey. Rodney the Wonder Squirrel. Bob the Robot. The Empress Eugenie. Adolph Menjou left me a cigar box containing his mustache.

And yet it is very lonely here on Zombie Island. We keep doing sequels. Return to Zombie Island. Revenge on Zombie Island. The Wolf Man on Zombie Island. That one had some redeeming artistic merit. Lon Chaney Junior has the eyes of a basset hound. The pathos is real, even when the dialogue sucks.

All of my attempts to escape from Zombie Island have met with humiliating failure. I had an offer to play King Lear in Pomona, but we were shooting the scene in which the Zombies devour Kate Smith that day. There is quicksand everywhere here. Carniverous gargoyles. Even the door knobs can speak.

Why are we making these unspeakable monstrosities, one after the other, you ask? What sort of cretin pays good money to watch them? Perhaps other zombies. Zombies from out of town, perhaps. But my theory is— nobody. The theatre is empty. We play in darkness, endlessly repeating, on a continuous loop to nowhere, for nobody, to no apparent purpose. This is the system of Doctor Sinistrari's personal hell.

Once I was greatly acclaimed as Richard the Third in Peterhead. Now I am a wrangler of zombies. Each hell is fashioned by its inhabitants. This is mine.

A zombie is dead and yet lives. Somewhere within the cramped boundaries of this absurd paradox lies whatever truth I own. This is the place where all contradictions are both necessary and true.

Wait. Do I hear the fog horn?

(He cups his hand to his ear first. Then, after a moment, the sound of the fog horn.)

Timing is everything. The excursion boat is here. Your devourer should be arriving shortly. Screaming is encouraged. Now. Let's all go out to the lobby to get some styrofoam popcorn and forty-seven year old hot dogs. The second show will be starting any minute. But don't be alarmed. It's exactly the same as the first.

There's the fog horn again.

(He cups his hand to his ear. Then the sound of the fog horn.)

Welcome to Zombie Island. I am the evil Doctor Sinistrari. I have locked you in my cabinet of horrors. It does not matter that Aquanetta cannot act. She is unspeakably beautiful.

(The light fades on him and goes out.)

THE RAT-CATCHER'S TALE

CHARACTERS

NANNY – an old woman

SETTING

She speaks from a small circle of light on an otherwise dark stage.

"It was first a slow, caressing sound, then more and more lively and urgent, and so sonorous and piercing that it penetrated the farthest alleys and retreats of the town where all could hear it.

Soon from the bottom of the cellars, the top of the garrets, from all the nooks and corners of the houses, out came the rats, flinging themselves into the street, and trip, trip, trip, beginning to run toward the front of the town hall, so squeezed together they flooded the pavement like the waves of a flooded torrent.

When the square was quite full the piper faced about and, still playing briskly, turned toward the river that runs at the foot of the walls of Hamelin."

–*Andrew Lang,* "The Red Fairy Book"

(From a circle of light on an otherwise dark stage,
NANNY, *an old woman, speaks.)*

NANNY. So you want a story, and you want a story, and you refuse to go to sleep without a story, you nasty little creatures. All right then. You shall have a story. But I must warn you, children, that a story can be a very dangerous animal indeed. But if you insist, upon a story, then a story you must have. And a very pretty story it is, too, with a very happy ending.

Once upon a time, long ago, when I was a little girl, the city of Hamelin was overrun with rats. Oh, children, there were rats everywhere. There were rats in the cellars and rats in the attics and rats in the cupboards and rats in the privies and rats in the church and rats in the town hall, rats, rats, rats everywhere, nibbling and squeaking and crawling and hanging and running and biting and hissing and scuttling, rats, rats, rats. They licked the soup from ladles and bit babies in their cradles, made nests in hats and ate the cats.

The people of Hamelin tried everything to get rid of the rats. They poisoned them, and trapped them, and stepped on them, and burned them, but for every rat they killed, there seemed to be a hundred more. It was a horrifying thing. We would go to sleep at night and dream of rats, and then wake up and rats were crawling on the bed and nibbling at our faces. It was a desperate situation, children.

Then one day, a stranger appeared in the town. He was a tall, stooped, sharp faced man in a piebald suit, with deep blue eyes and a pipe in his knapsack. This odd looking stranger made his way to the town hall and informed the mayor that for a considerable fee he would guarantee to rid the town of all the rats. And as the stranger spoke, his long, twisted fingers moved like spiders at the end of his hands, as if they were trying to crawl away from him. It was an enormous fee the rat-catcher demanded, but the people were desperate, and so the mayor swore to pay.

So the rat-catcher stood in the center of town, before the town hall, with an odd little smile on his face, and he took his pipe from out of his knapsack, and he began to play.

(As she speaks, we hear the song of the pipe.)

Quietly, at first. An eerie song, a mournful thing, a song that seemed at once so strange and yet familiar, as if it were a song I'd heard when I was somebody else, in a time before I was born, someplace in a dream, in another story I lived before I was a little girl in Hamelin.

And at first there was nothing. Just the eerie music. And then there was a rustling, and then a squeaking, and then one rat appeared, its nose sniffing the air, confused, uncertain, and then another, and then another, and then the rats began to come. One, and then three, and then seven, then dozens of rats, hundreds of rats, thousands of rats, brown rats, black rats, gray rats, streaming down the cobbled alleys, down the rainspouts, up the basement steps, out of sheds and up out of wells, the rats came, thousands and thousands of rats, the square was an ocean of rats, we were all running to climb onto wagons and walls to escape them, so many rats, uncountable rats, a slithering, squeaking carpet of rats, an ocean of rats, rats, rats, all drawn to the piper's music.

And then the piper began to walk from the town square towards the river, still playing his pipe as he walked, and the rats followed him, and when he came to the river he walked into the water and stood, a few feet from the bank, and the rats began to follow him into the river, rat after rat after rat, hopping into the water, plop, plop, plop, thousands and thousands of rats, all into the water, until there was just one rat left, the

Queen of the Rats, an enormous, enormous rat, who glared at the piper as if she'd known him in another life, then jumped into the river after the rest.

(The music ends.)

And the people of Hamelin cheered, and hoisted the rat-catcher up on their shoulders, and carried him to the town square, where they put him down before the mayor, and the piper demanded his fee. And the mayor looked at the piper, and smiled and said, Surely you didn't really believe we had the sum you asked for. We were desperate, and you saved us, and we're grateful. Now, take this handful of pennies and go.

You swore, said the rat-catcher, staring at the mayor with his bright blue eyes. You swore to pay what I asked if I removed the vermin from the town.

Don't be a troublesome fellow, said the mayor. Take these pennies with our thanks, and go.

And the rat-catcher bowed, a strange little bow, and said he would collect his fee at a later time, and walked away, and all the good people of Hamelin congratulated the mayor on making such a shrewd bargain.

And that night, when the people of Hamelin were asleep, the rat-catcher walked into the dark and empty town square of Hamelin, and took up his pipe again, and once again began to play his eerie song.

(sound of the music again)

And the mayor stirred in his sleep, and thought, how strange, that the rat-catcher should play in the night, when there were no more rats in all of Hamelin town. But then the people began to notice that their children were getting out of bed, and walking down the halls and out of the houses, walking to the town square, hundreds and hundreds of children, all the children of the town, drawn by the music. And then the piper began to walk, out of the town, and over the bridge, towards the mountain, and all the children followed him, and he led them to a cave in the mountainside, and all the children marched into the cave, and when they were all inside, the earth collapsed, and the cave was closed, and the children trapped in a cavern deep inside the mountain.

(The music stops.)

And inside the mountain it was very dark. The children could hear the rush and gurgle of the river flowing through the cavern, and farther away, the sounds of their parents digging, trying desperately to reach them, but the more they dug, the more earth would collapse. And inside the mountain, deep in the dark, the children could see, there in the darkness, what looked to them like pairs of little red lights. Two. Then two more. Then two more, then more and more until the cave seemed to be entirely full of these little red lights, like Christmas lights.

Then the children saw that the red lights were the glowing eyes of the rats, hundreds of rats, thousands of rats, hungry rats, glaring at them in the dark, for the rats had swum up the river that flowed deep under the mountainside, into the cavern. And the rats were very hungry. And so the rats began to eat. And they ate and ate and ate. And the people of Hamelin could hear the horrible, horrible screams of the children from deep within the mountainside, but when they finally dug out the cave in the morning, and made their way to the caverns, all they could find were a great many little piles of bones.

There, children. Now wasn't that a nice story? Aren't you happy you begged your poor old Nanny for a story? But children, I must tell you now, that is not quite the end of the story. Because I am not your old Nanny. I look like your old Nanny, but in fact the rats have eaten her, and saved the skin, and crawled inside the skin, and when I take off my skin, you will see me for who I am, for I am the Queen of the Rats, and I have brought all my subjects here to meet you, and when we're done eating our supper, I promise, you'll never want any more stories, ever again. And in the morning when your mother comes to wake you, all she'll find is a little pile of bones.

(**NANNY** *makes a little choking noise. Then another, louder. She puts her hands up to her mouth. A third choking noise. Then a rather horrible squeaking noise is heard. When she pulls her hands away, we can see the head of a squeaking rat beginning to emerge from her mouth. Blackout. Sound of squeaking in the darkness.*)

PRODUCTION NOTE FOR
THE RAT-CATCHER'S TALE:

Under no circumstances should a live rat ever be used in this production. No performer should ever put any rat, alive or dead, in their mouth. Use the head of a rubber rat, or a rat fashioned of some edible or non-toxic material, concealed in the garments of the performer, and placed in her mouth when she puts her hands up there at the end. She should be able to make the rat squirm a bit by moving it with her tongue. Make sure the rat is too big to be swallowed or choked on. The safety and comfort of the performer should not be compromised in any way in any production of this play.

PSALMS OF SCATTERED BONES

CHARACTERS

OLIVE – a waitress

SETTING

She speaks to us sitting at a table in a restaurant, after closing time.

Every one of them is gone back:
they are altogether become filthy;
there is none that doeth good,
no, not one.

Have the workers of iniquity no knowledge?
who eat up my people as they eat bread:
they have not called upon God.

There were they in great fear,
where no fear was:
for God hath scattered the bones…

Psalm 53

(**OLIVE**, *a waitress, speaks from a table at a restaurant. It's after closing time. Perhaps the occasional sounds of dishes and glasses clinking and running water in the background.*)

OLIVE. He was vain. Always talking himself up,
   like he was trying to prove something
   to somebody. Not me.
   Some other person who wasn't there.

   He carried an old fashioned straight razor.
   I asked him, Did you kill a barber to get that?

   Maybe, he said. I don't remember
   what he was.

   He was a liar. I liked that about him.
   I used to laugh when he made love to me.
   He hated that.
   He couldn't understand
   that I was laughing
   because it made me happy.

   He didn't believe in God.
   Or at least he didn't like him much.
   And he didn't think much of people either.

   Nobody is good, he said. Not one.
   And nobody is saved.
   This is Hell right here, he said.
   We're all in Hell,
   and we just don't know it.

   Some day you're going to take that razor,
   I said to him,
   and ventilate my throat.

Maybe, he said.

I was pretty young, but I could tell
he was mostly bluster and bullshit.
I liked that. It made him seem
vulnerable.

And the sex was exciting.
Hot flesh. I remember
hot flesh. The passion
was real. He needed me.

Every day when I'd walk to the restaurant
I passed this old weird house.
The front yard was a mess.
The garden in back was worse.
I walked past the house
then turned left at the corner
and walked along a falling apart fence
between the garden and the sidewalk.

And I'd look up over the fence
and there at the window
at the top of the house
the old man would be looking out at me.

The glass was dirty, but I could make out
a big wild shock of white hair.
Craggy face covered in stubble.
An old stained tee shirt,
the kind without sleeves.

And long, gnarled arms, and big hands.
The old man was there every day
when I walked to work.
And every night when I walked home,
no matter how late it was,
there he'd be at the window,
in a dim lit frame in the dark,
looking out at me.

And sometimes I could hear
from somewhere back in the house
what sounded like an old player piano
out of key and skipping parts,
playing some old love song, or a hymn.

And sometimes I could smell
something cooking in the house.
Some stew meat or some such thing.

And I got so I looked forward
to seeing the old man at the window
when I went by.
I liked the sound of the piano
and the smell of something cooking.

I would look up at the old man
in the window
and he would look at me
and I'd walk by.

I used to tease Jacob.
I told him I had another admirer.
I told him about the old man.
And sometimes he'd walk me home at night
and look up at that window
and see the old man looking down at us.
He hated that old man.

I told him, Jacob, what's the harm?
He's just an old man
in an old house
who likes to look out the window
at a girl going by.

But Jacob hated him.
I should kill that son of a bitch, he said.
That old man.
The way he looks at you.

I bet you he's got money, Jacob said.
I bet you he's got money in that house.
The filthy son of a bitch.

It got so it was all he'd talk about.
That old man. How that old man
kept looking at me through the window.
How he bet the old man had
tons of money stuffed in dresser drawers.

One night he said, let's kill him.
Kill who? I said.
We were naked in bed.
Let's kill that old man, he said.
And take his money.

You're crazy, I said.
I mean it, he said.
We could do it and make a new life.
Get out of this town.

Jacob was all bluff, I told myself.
He didn't really mean it.
It just made the sex more exciting,
to talk about doing something
bad and dangerous.

But one night he was walking me home.
The wind was blowing.
Clouds running past the moon.
There was a little break in the fence
just before you got to the place
where the old man could see you
walking towards the corner,
along the garden.

And Jacob pulled me back in the shadows
and kissed me hard.
Tonight's the night, he said.

What night? I said.

The night we kill the old man, he said.
He was running his hands up and down my
thighs and buttocks and I was getting
very aroused, just at the edge of
exhausted but with my senses
thrilling with the wind and the dark
and the danger.

He pulled me through the break
in the fence and into the shadows
of the ruined garden.
It was very dark.
He laid me down on a little
grassy place and took my clothes off,
then made desperate, tender
animal love to me.
I was shuddering and shuddering.
Then he held me and I fell asleep.

I half woke, hearing him whisper in my dream
that he'd be back with the money.
Then I slept again.

When I woke up it was very early morning,
and I was lying in the garden,
naked and very cold.
I opened my eyes and looked up
at the house and there at the window
I saw the old man looking out at me.

Our eyes met. He had no expression on
his face that I could read, but those eyes,
staring at me, lying on my back there naked,
those eyes that looked through me to the
back of my head.

It was like I was hypnotized.

I got up and scrambled around for my clothes and ran,
dressing in a hurry in the shadow of the wall,
then ran home.

Jacob wasn't there.
He wasn't anywhere.
I never saw him again.
He left all his things.

I left town and never went back.
To this day I don't know
what happened.

But I keep remembering two things
about that morning.
One was the smell of cooking from the house.
The smell of roasting flesh.

The other was that, when I looked around me
in the ruined garden in the light of day,
I could see that scattered everywhere
were hundreds and hundreds of bones.

(The light fades on her and goes out.)

EVENT HORIZON

CHARACTERS

THE CAPTAIN – a middle-aged man in what is apprently a pilot's uniform

SETTING

He speaks to the audience from a chair in a circle of light on an otherwise dark stage.

ABOUT THIS PLAY

EVENT HORIZON was first presented by the Drove Theatre Company at the Greenwich Street Theatre in New York City on February 11, 2006. The performance was directed by Marc Bertha, with costumes by David Withrow. The cast was as follows:

THE CAPTAIN . . . . Sean Sutherland

(A circle of light on **THE CAPTAIN,** *a man who is wearing what looks something like a commercial pilot's uniform, but we can't be sure. It might be the future, or it might not be. He speaks into a small object which he relates to as if it were a pilot's intercom, but which in fact may be an old electric razor. He might have been drinking, but if so, he holds it pretty well.)*

THE CAPTAIN. Folks, this is your Captain speaking. We'll be arriving shortly at the Event Horizon, from which nothing can return. If you want to take a look out the windows, on either side you can see the black hole swallowing up a variety of objects. There goes a white dwarf. There goes a Buick. And there goes a cow. Good night, Elsie. Please keep your seat belts fastened and your trays in the locked and upright position. Please turn off all devices. No devices of any sort will be operational once we have passed the Event Horizon. We should be reaching the end of the observable universe in just a few moments.

You might want to take this opportunity to consume the last of your alcoholic beverages, or take a moment to remember a loved one, because on the other side of the Event Horizon there is no memory and no going back. All constructions will be deconstructed there. All hopes will end. All fears will prove to have been either correct, irrelevant, or both. So sit back, relax, and enjoy the inexorable plunge into the singularity where all choices terminate.

I might add that it's possible that all information crossing the Event Horizon is somehow recorded there, although it's unclear how anybody could go about retrieving it, and doing so would most likely only produce a cold, pale ghost of what we usually think of as reality, much like my first marriage.

And yet, it may give you a certain amount of satisfaction to know that recorded there somewhere within the Event Horizon, like the remains of a deserted library on the windswept Mongolian plains, are the private letters of James Knox Polk, the little blue cowboy records you had as a child, the entire contents of Howard Pyle's attic, circa 1910, the dental records of twenty thousand murdered Lithuanian children, the blueprints for the farmhouse of Mrs Bessie Potdorf of 412 Armitage Avenue, Armitage, Ohio, a complete set of Mad Comics, your grandmother's lost cat, the Tasmanian Encyclopedia of Ichthyology, a box of prophylactics from the planet Zordack, Marilyn Monroe's missing diary, the cherry colored pocket knife your father lost while playing football in the street in 1934, naked pictures of Leonid Brezhnev, eleven previously unknown plays of Shakespeare, the bones of the prophet Ezekiel, and every creature you ever loved.

I know what each and every one of you is thinking at this moment. You're thinking, why didn't I have more sexual intercourse when I had the chance? And the answer is, you probably wouldn't have enjoyed it all that much anyway. The whole thing would have been over before you knew what was happening, like everything else in your life. And yet, that being said, on a more personal note, I sincerely want to thank your Flight Attendant, Sally, for that magical layover we spent in Toledo. The last thing I think about, Sally, before the lights go out, will be your wonderfully soft, cock-eyed breasts.

The temperature at our destination is only slightly above absolute zero, so baggage claim is probably not something you'll need to worry about. And I can't tell you what time it is, because my watch has stopped, but it doesn't make much difference, since where we're going, space is reduced to one dimension, and time expands into three, making past, present and future simultaneous in any direction, so theoretically you should be able to regret things even before they happen, much like my second marriage.

I've enjoyed being your pilot, at least about thirteen percent of the time, when I was conscious, although I must confess I've never been completely certain what the hell I was doing. What are all these damned gadgets and doohickeys for, anyway? Did we really need all this crap to get here? And why does everybody always have to change in Pittsburgh? Although the pizza there is very good. I wish I had some now. And why do all the mechanics and baggage handlers have that same glassy look in their eyes, like the speed freaks I knew in college? Do they know something I don't? And why have I spent my entire life suffocating in a perpetual state of dread?

The truth is, folks, you've always been completely at the mercy of circumstances that are mostly out of your control and far beyond your comprehension. So why should plunging over a cosmic precipice into catastrophic oblivion feel much different from your basic Tuesday in Terre Haute? We've always lived at the edge of an abyss. The darkness has always surrounded us. Armageddon is omnipresent. Every day is Judgement Day. Every betrayal is a fragment of the Apocalypse. So my advice, children, is, since you're probably never going to know what hit you anyway, when you get a chance, you might as well just put that nipple in your mouth, close your eyes, and suck for all you're worth. But like all the good advice you've ever gotten, I'm giving it to you when it's too late to do you any good.

So, on behalf of the entire crew, we hope you've had a pleasant journey. And in the unlikely event that there actually is something on the other side of the Event Horizon, please make your way down the worm hole in an orderly fashion to your next point of embarkation. Good luck, and thank you for—

(blackout)